Also by the author:

Vanilla Gorilla
Llamas in the Laundry
Dream Helmet

The Year I was Grounded

by William New

Vancouver
London

Distribution and representation in Canada by
Fitzhenry & Whiteside • www.fitzhenry.ca

Distribution and representation in the UK by
Turnaround • www.turnaround-uk.com

Released in USA Spring 2009

Mixed Sources
Cert no. SW-COC-001271
© 1996 FSC
FSC

Inside pages printed on FSC certified paper using vegetable-based inks.

Manufactured by Sunrise Printing
Manufactured in Chilliwack, BC, Canada in June 2010

2 4 6 8 10 9 7 5 3

Cataloguing-in-Publication Data for this book
is available from The British Library.

Library and Archives Canada Cataloguing in Publication

New, W. H. (William Herbert), 1938-
The year I was grounded / William H. New.

Poems.
ISBN 978-1-896580-35-7

1. Children's poetry, Canadian (English). I. Title.

PS8577.E776Y33 2008   jC811'.54   C2008-902866-X

This book is for Gareth

—W.N.

Tradewind Books thanks the Governments of Canada and British Columbia for the financial support they have extended through the Canada Book Fund, Livres Canada Books, the Canada Council for the Arts, the British Columbia Arts Council and the British Columbia Book Publishing Tax Credit program.

Canada Council for the Arts   Conseil des Arts du Canada

BRITISH COLUMBIA ARTS COUNCIL
Supported by the Province of British Columbia

Canada

LIVRES CANADA BOOKS

WINTER

Every January

   my granddad says

      Winter: under January snow
      the earth does not sleep,
      it churns with dreaming:

      roots tingle at the prospect of May,
      woodchucks mumble,
      seeds jostle like people sweeping—

      if you listen, you won't hear them:
      they'll go still—
      you can't eavesdrop on dreams

My Journal, January 6th

My grandma and granddad gave me this journal to write in. I said, "What will I write?" and Grandma said, "Geordie, dear"—I ask her not to call me "dear" all the time, but secretly I'm sort of glad she does anyway—"just write down all the things you like and all the things you don't like," so here goes:

Things I Like	Things I Don't Like
baseball	liver
playing the trumpet	people getting angry
swimming	
anything to do with water	
toasted cheese sandwiches	
broccoli	
crunching raw carrots	
fish	
numbers and lines	
dill pickles	
skateboarding	
singing	
kayaking	
drawing	
anything to do with snow	
spiders	
computer games	
chocolate cake	

I like lists, too.

And lemonade.   But not beans.

Getting Grounded

Some days I'm all thumbs when I play the trumpet.

Some days the pictures I draw don't look like anything at all.

And some days, playing baseball, I trip over my own feet.

When my brother plays hockey or bows the double bass, and when my sister plays soccer or pounds on the drums, *they* always seem to know where *their* hands and feet are.

Not me.

My mum and dad say not to worry. It's just because I'm growing, they say.

Getting stronger, too.

Except *getting stronger* sometimes gets me into trouble—like this week, for instance, when I was

> throwing a ball outside,
> I smashed a window—no place to hide—
>
> I heard my dad thundering "WHO BROKE THE GLASS? WHO CAUSED THAT CLATTERING BATTERING CRASH?"

I forgot who I was.

"Not me," I croaked.

He was holding the ball.

"Ida-Know. Just broke."

I tried to look blameless.
I opened wide eyes.

Dad lifted an eyebrow.

"Maybe some guys?"

"Well," he replied, "You can take The Guys with you,
Ida, Not-Me, and Just-Broke,

and until you can find your way back once again
to Yourself, You're Grounded. Do I need to explain?"

No, he didn't. At all. But I grumbled and groaned,
and mumbled and moped like a sick saxophone.

"We love you," he added, "all day, every night—
and in darkness or light, when you're you,
you're just right."

My Journal, January 10th

"We love you," Dad said.

Yeah.

I still had to help him fix the window pane.

And I'm not allowed to do any fun things for Two Whole Weeks. I have to stay Close to Home. No treats. No Backtalk. No Computer Games.

Replacing the window pane was sort of interesting, though. I didn't know that glass was made of sand.

And at least Mum and Dad aren't angry with me. Actually, I don't think they ever were. Just annoyed at me for trying to hide.

"When you're You, you're just right," Dad said.

OK.

But who am I? It could take me a whole year to figure that one out.

Maybe more.

Thinking Fast

Some days my brain turns somersaults
and ideas tumble head over heliotrope

Whirlwinds rampage,
and if I happen to be thinking of a field of cows,
suddenly they'll all be running,
the brown ones in front of the black-and-white ones,
running towards a purple hill
with a purple lake on the far side

and all the cows will turn somersaults
except one, who will travel by whirlwind
down to the pebbly lakeshore,
and be already sipping lemonade
by the time the others roll up breathless

grass-covered,
       grinning,
            and green

My Journal, February 10th

It snowed again last week but today the sun was shining and the sky was bright blue, so my friends and I built a snow fort in the park where we usually play baseball in the spring. We built two forts actually and pelted snowballs at each other—and at my brother and sister, too. My sister threw a really good one—she got me right on the nose!!! We laughed all afternoon and panted so hard we were steaming like volcanoes. And then one of my friends lost a glove and my sister lost her hat, and by the time we found them our hands were cold, so we went home and my mum was making hot chocolate for everybody. She said we had to solve this word puzzle first—

"Easy," I said, "that's Hot Chocolate with Milk in it!" And it was.

Then we played computer games for a while, conquering dragons and searching for hidden treasure till the dark came all too soon. I think I now have electronic thumbs.

At dinner, my dad looked at me and said, "As you like raw carrots so much, let's try growing some." So later on he hauls out the seed catalogue, and I like the sound of the variety they call _Bolero_—they taste sweet and crunchy and are good for snacking, the catalogue says. _75 days to harvest_. Or maybe _Mokum_—crisp and munchable, _56 days_. By the time they'll be ready to eat I'll be half a year older.

I like writing poems and sometimes I type them up on my granddad's old typewriter.

My granddad told me he tried snowboarding once but thought he should have started a long time ago.

Monday Mealtime

Friday: I'm so hungry
I could eat a chocolate cake.

> "Hmmm," said my mum,
> "Stomach ache."

Saturday: so hungry
I could eat an overcoat.

> "Hmmm," said my mum,
> "Sore throat."

Sunday: I could swallow
all the fish in every river.

> "Good," said my mum,
> "We're having liver."

"YUCK," I said, "LIVER! Never ever liver please!
I'll eat a head of broccoli, a loaf of toast and cheese,
I'll even eat the pickle jar—unless it's filled with beans—"
but then I stopped—I realized
that I was being teased,

so beans, I grinned,
beans:

I'm so hungry,
even beans
might taste OK,
if peeled.

> "Too late," mum laughed.
> "I've made instead
> your favourite Monday meal!"

My Journal, March 1st

Did I also say I like WORD PUZZLES and
WORDS? Well I do. I don't like how words

STumblE sometimes, but I like how you
can make them

SHOUT their way across the
page, or

wriggle
into
small
corners

or sometimes rhyme, like slime, or a grimy
slimy lime-green dime—which I could hang
on a wind-chime—over my brother's bed—
BUFFLEHEAD!!!

I still don't like beans.

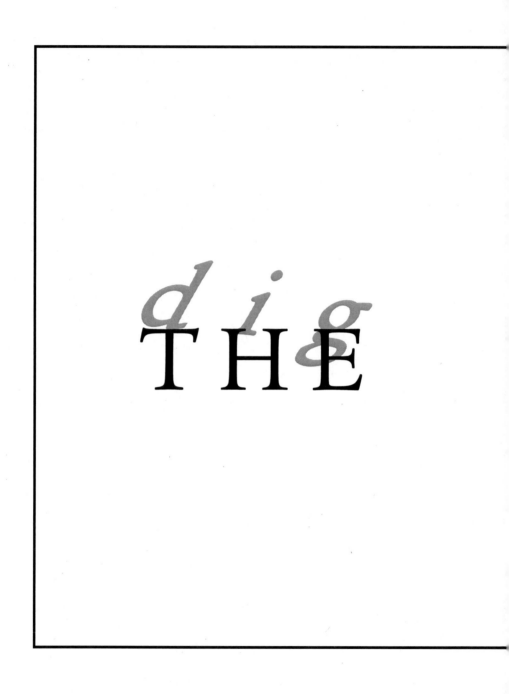

EARTH

Animal Ramble

The animals that ramble the earth
do not walk identically:

elephants **LUMBER**,

blue peacocks strut,

STAMPEDING caribou

TRAMP distance into dust.

Maybe young moles are taught
digging dances—

rhumbas and sambas—

while overhead a Persian kitten *gambols*
in feathery grass,
and small ocelots practise slow S T A L K ING:

here, a knot of **WRITHING** adders:

there, a GREEN RUSH of salamanders:

while on the street,

a **CRUSH** of climbing boots and running shoes,

a trot of heels and buckled tongues—

who knows
how they will j u m p about among bare toes?

SPRING

Every April

   my grandma says

      In April, in the rain,

      when daffodils shine
      in the neighbours' window-boxes,

      and baseball diamonds beckon,
      where even the moon is melting the snow,

      you're shivering spring

Band Practice

My sister is a *RAT*
I mean a *RAT-a-TAT-TAT*,
she's a drummer she's a
RAT-a-THAT'S THAT!

      (*RAT-a-TAT*)

and a *bass* and a *bass* and a *bass* and a *bass*,
you can hear when my brother strums along—

      (*RAT-a-TAT*)

there's a *note*, then a *slide*,
then a *smooth bass glide*,
when the *bass* hums its *double-bass* song—

      (*RAT-a-TAT*)

But **NOW**
    THINK
    FREE!

      (*Rat-a*)

**LISTEN
TO
ME!**

(Rat-a)

THAT'S what
I say
when**EVER** it is that
I play—

'Cos like it or lump it
I have a pet trumpet—

**THINK FAST—
IT'S A BLAST!**

*(RAT-a-ta-
TA-ta-ta-
TAT)*

Breathing

Some people breathe air quietly.
Some snore.

Some houses breathe dampness
in and out, like sponges.

Plastic
doesn't breathe at all.

My next-door neighbour
breathes fire.

You can see it in her nostrils
when she inhales, and then

Out honks "**STOP THAT NOISE,
GO SOMEWHERE ELSE,**

TURN DOWN THAT WHADDAYACALLIT!"

She's combustible—

But my grandma
breathes slowly.

When she plays computer games, bakes chocolate cake,
solves puzzles, makes lemonade

and listens to our band practice after school,
she murmurs,

"That's nice dear" and "What happens
Next?" and "Aren't you clever!"

Oxygen

I do not think about the air.
I breathe because it's always there.

But what if it wasn't?

Aren't there rules,
regulations, molecules

(maybe even microscopic)
to bring it safely back, or stop it

turning soupy greasy grey?

(Isn't the air still here today?)

I'm having trouble sorting out
the lines dividing truth and doubt.

All I want is what I need—
I want my breathing guaranteed.

breathing and

breathing

My Journal, May 1st

I saw two little kids this week riding sidewalk-cars in front of our house, just like I used to do a long time ago. The cars were shaped like fire engines, and the kids were screaming siren-noises *EE-OO-EE-OO-EE-OO-EE* and you could see that they thought they were going faster than the wind. Dreaming of being firefighters, I bet. Or maybe cowboys with firemen's hats, because sometimes they were shouting *RIDE-'EM, EE-OO, BANG!* Then they stopped at the corner, turned around, and pedalled like crazy back to where they'd started from.

I was on my skateboard, practising ollies and kickflips at the curb. One of my friends was there with me, and maybe in a couple of years we're going to go pro. I know you can do it. We've seen it on tv.

The carrot seed arrived in the mail. My dad and I are going to plant it on May 24th.

Spider Games

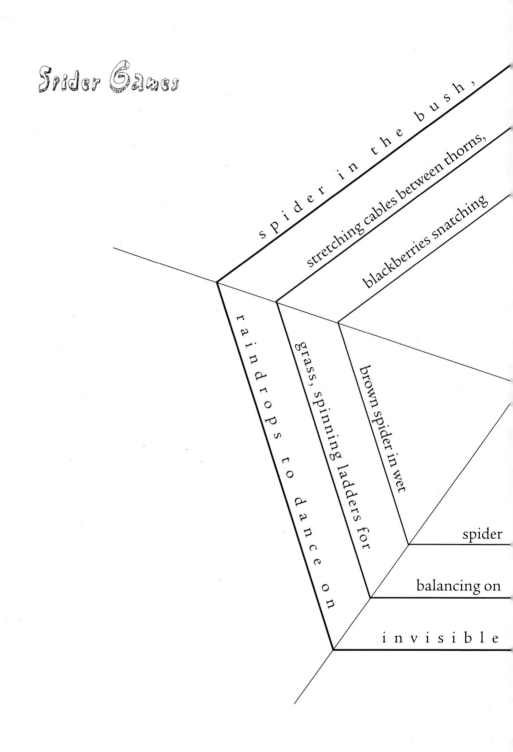

spider in the bush,
stretching cables between thorns,
blackberries snatching
brown spider in wet
grass, spinning ladders for
raindrops to dance on
spider
balancing on
invisible

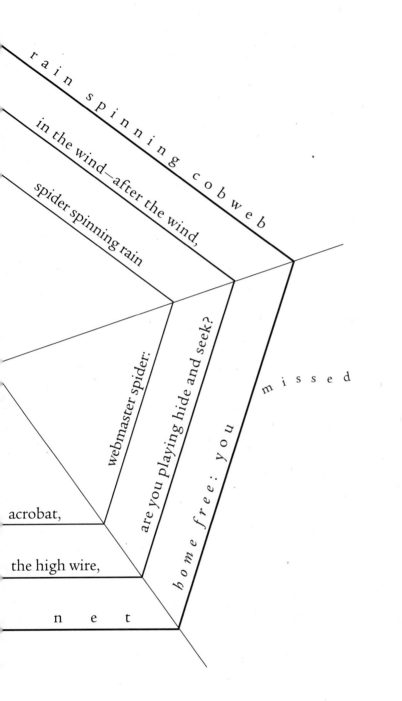

rain spinning cobweb

in the wind—after the wind,

spider spinning rain

webmaster spider:

are you playing hide and seek?

home free: you

missed

me

acrobat,

the high wire,

n e t

Air Song

Some days I try to imagine Air's point-of-view
      living free
      gallivanting after kites
      and holding up birds' wings

I figure sights like these belong to Air
      giving lift to jumbo jets and hawks
      quivering high-jumpers tensing for more height
      slow stratus and streaking cirrus
      white, with a storm on the way
      shivering the blue

Look at the wind

It's only Air cavorting
tumbling ten top hats along the sidewalk
lolloping, rollicking, crooning

Air wanting freedom back
from where it's caught in inner tubes
and red balloons

Air keening
through windowcracks and doors
sighing

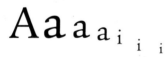

Aaa a i   i   i   r   r   r

My Journal, June 1st

We had band practice at school this morning
and instead of skreeking and skrawking and
missing the high notes the way we usually do
when we start up, we actually sounded pretty
good. The tubas and drums were all thumping
when they were supposed to thump and quiet
when they were supposed to be quiet, and
the flutes and clarinets stayed mostly in tune.
We were playing the 007 theme and I had
a solo and I really blasted it! I think I woke
up every cat and dog within twenty blocks.
HEAR THEM HOWL!!!

My dad gave me another word puzzle last
week. It looked like this:

_____ment
sub_____ment
_____ball
_____board
(2nd, 1st)_____man

Took me a while, but I figured out the
answer, which is sort of funny. Like my dad.
When my friends ask me what my dad is
like, I say:

Some people keep carp
in their garden pond.
My dad keeps
crocodiles.

"Herons don't bother them," he says,
"and raccoons stay clear in the night
when they dance the cucuracha
and play cards."

"They play a mean game of Snap,"
my dad says.

Then he grins.

My mum shakes her head when he says things
like this. But he says them anyway.

Tonight, out of the blue, he said, "You'll have
to weed the carrots, you know." Then a
bit later he added, "And you're in charge of
keeping the carrot flies away."

Even though the carrots aren't exactly
growing yet.

SUMMER

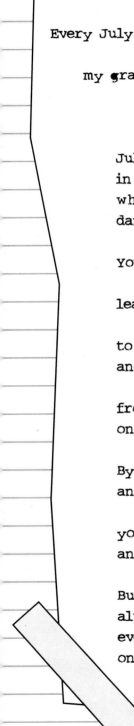

Every July

   my grandma says

      July,
      in the night,
      when the rainbirds
      dance on the roof and under the eaves

      you'll dream there's a chance you can join
          them,
      leave your bed and fly, high as make-believe
          castletops,
      to hunt for summer treasure—
      and when you get there you'll retrieve silver
          coins
      from caches in the night,
      on the roof and under the eaves

      By day, when you're awake again
      and the trance has evaporated just like
          steam,
      you'll maybe grieve for parched dreams
      and lost expanse

      But remember this:
      always you can weave them back,
      every night when the rainbirds dance
      on the roof and under the eaves

My Journal, June 23rd

Some of the Things I Like About Summer

I get to go the lake and go swimming,
and this year maybe go kayaking too.

No school.

I get to play every day in the sunshine.

If it rains I can still draw, or play in the
band, or toast a cheese sandwich when I
get hungry, or try to figure out some
more puzzles.

Baseball of course.

Some of the Things I Like About Little League

You have to warm up and you have to
cool down, and in between you play play
play, yell "Hey Batter Hey Batter," and
everyone's Alive.

Coach shouting "You can do it" and "Way to Go, Kid!"

Just the excitement of hitting the ball—maybe hitting a double—and running running running running running and sliding into 2nd base safe.

The *thwack* of the bat, the *buzz* of the crowd, the *plock* of the ball when it lands in my glove, the *whoosh* of a fast pitch.

And the noise the crowd makes, too. My brother and sister and mum and dad and grandma and granddad all there at the game, waving and cheering.

And everyone singing the Ball Game Song, most of them off-key. But LOUD! Are they EVER LOUD!

Hotdogs. Mustard. Peanuts. Popsicles.
Triple-flavour ice cream. Fizzy cold
lemonade.

Yesterday—last inning—we needed one
more run to win. Only one out.
Runners on second and third, and my
turn at bat. Coach signals me to swing
on the first pitch. I hit a grounder.
But guess what? Baseball's really crazy
sometimes. The fielder fumbled the ball
and tossed it to first instead of home
plate. Big mistake. I was out. But it
didn't matter 'cos the runner on third
scored. We won, and I got an RBI!

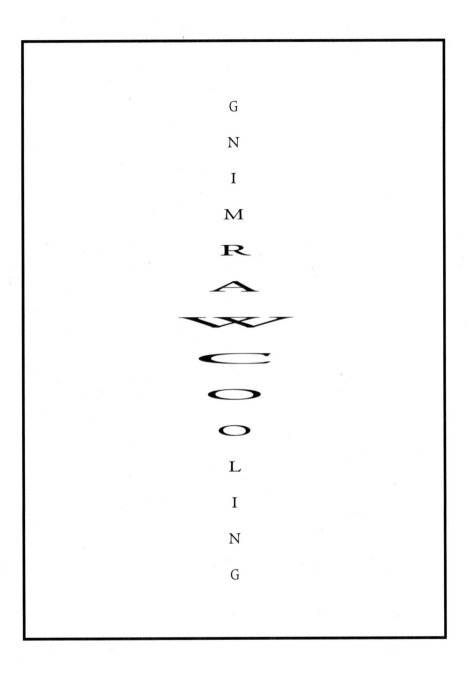

Getting Granddad to Swim

My granddad says
that he'll come in
and join us
for a little swim—

"unless the water's wet again"

He puts on snorkel,
goggles, fins,
and says he really
will come in—

"unless the water's wet again"

We tell him "NO—
this year it's dry!
The waves are crisp—
this is JULY!"

So he comes in
and makes a fuss
because it's wet,
and he laughs with us—

the way he always does—

Nothing ever changes here.
I love it 'cos it's warm and clear—

swimming in the lake

putting

T b H o E t h

W f A e T e E t R

Draw Fish

Fish flicker,
catch the last light to reach the trout pool,
the unrippled river's-edge
where rainbows gather:

slight
sudden flicks of fin and tail
stipple the surface—

        fish
           nibbling mosquito larvae,
           evening flies alighting:

each flicker shimmers,
as though scribbling colour
to stave off the closing night.

Do you see them in your mind's eye?

Hear gnats and water gliders dancing the border
between water and air?

Do you ever wish you lived where rainbows grow?

I do

I dream up pictures, braid colour
into flicker, shimmer, pool

I draw

My Journal, July 15th

The carrots have sprouted in the garden.
Already we can thin out some of the baby
ones.

```
ca      r  r  ot   s   car   ro     tsc      arr
CA         R  O    S   CA    R      TS       A R
CA            O    S   CA    R      T        A R
C                      A     R               R
```

Sweet.

otscarr otsweedcarro ts

OT C OT WEED RO TS

O C T R S

O T S

Summer

In August we go to the lake,
my dad and I

he tells me stories of when he was little
and granddad took him to the lake
and told him stories

I wonder if it's the same fish
still swimming there, with grey beard
and serious eyes

and if the laughter that bubbles up
every morning
started long ago, before I was born,

and if it's only now that I hear it,
where sun's rays shimmer on the water
and slow waves lap upon the shore

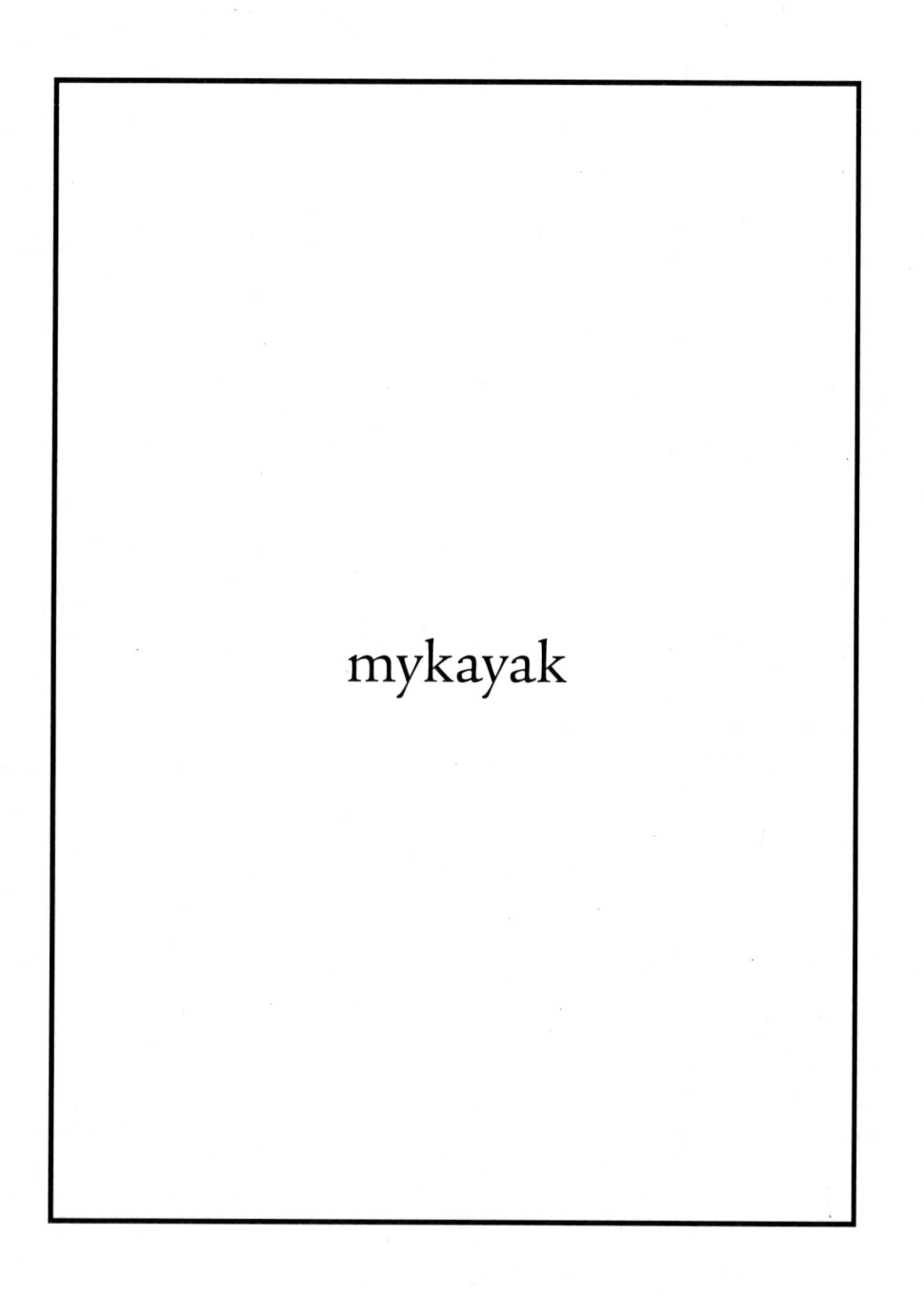

mykayak

THEL∃ꓘOЯTƧAKE

Matches

"Don't play with matches," my mother said,
when I was little,
"You'll blow us all to Smithereens—"

I didn't understand.
I thought Smithereens
was the name of a mountaintop

somewhere north of San Francisco, Nome, or Montreal,
and wondered what it would be like to visit,
if you could swim there, how far you could see.

One day I found it,
on the far side of wherever I'd been.
It wasn't fun.

Everyone was watching television,
day and night, day and night.
No-one was singing, not even their own songs.

The television news showed pictures
of earthquake fires, tsunami, floods,
ash from abrupt volcanoes, and people gasping.

I want to put things back the way they were.
It isn't possible.
Even the line between earth and sea

isn't firm, and who would expect explosions
to fall from the sky.

I wanted to plant a garden at the border,

reassemble broken houses—swim—
I wanted to help put out the fires,
and find a way to sing around the world.

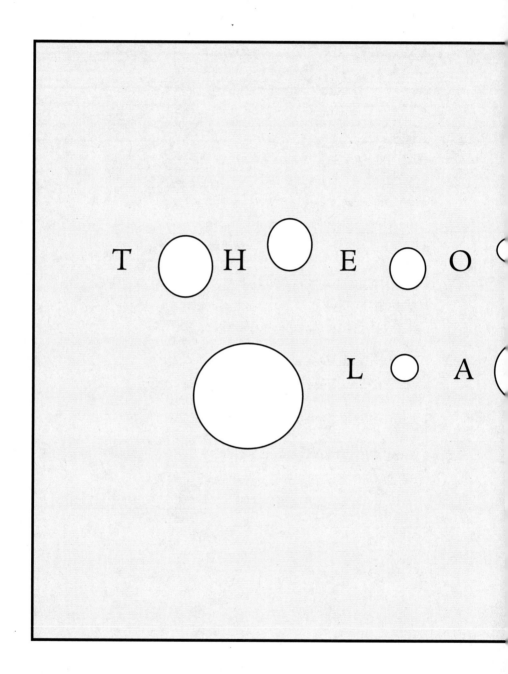

Z O N E

Y E R.

My Journal, August 27th

This week I've been finding out things I'm not sure I wanted to know. Stuff about dust. What it's made of. How dust turns into dust.

I found out that 18,000 mites can live in a single gram of dust. And when you breathe dust, you're breathing in dirt, coal ash, microscopic particles, lint, flour, feathers, fur, pet dander, interstellar specks, pollution, volcanic spew, and discarded skin.

Maybe 70% of house dust is made up of skin cells.

Life is complicated.

And facts don't always help you understand.

We said goodbye to Granddad this week.

I don't feel much like writing right now.

Dust to Dust

I figure dust is what you don't see
until the sun shines through a window

or what you don't notice
till a helicopter stirs up the ground

and under the blades a small cyclone
rages

I mean,
it seems too small to pay attention to

        but I'm pretty sure
        dust has plans

it's gathering in lumpy armies
under beds, invading lettuce leaves and eyes,

designing desert dunes in 4-by-40 barleyfields,
and taking over the world

the emperor of dust is a draft of air,
who moves mountains, particle by particle,

into thicknesses you can write your name in,
the size of empty lots and broken wings

When I'm Lonely

When I'm lonely I walk along the north beach
and watch the surf hammer rocks and barnacles—

and when the tide goes out, I imagine
floating on the last wave over the edge of the world,

following sun, moon, stars
to every shore of the ocean:

Honshu, Ellesmere, the Balearic Islands

I am like the wind—
explorer,

living free—

and by the time the tide returns,
I am no longer alone

I ride the surf shoreward,
singing

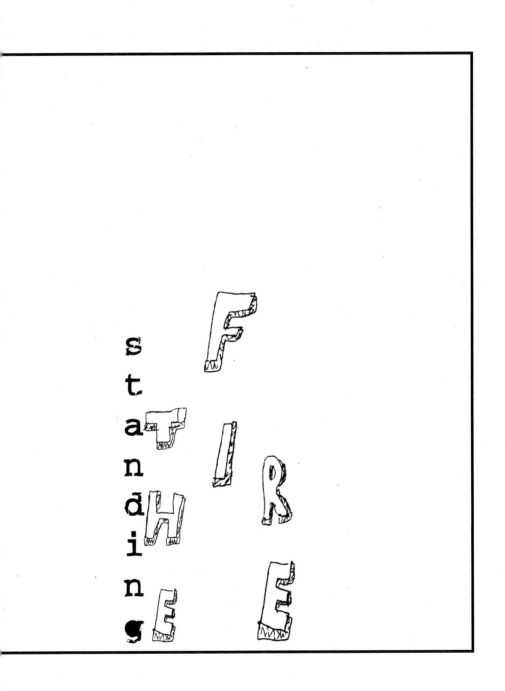

September – My Grandma's Fire Song

Late one summer evening, by the shore,
we sing old songs and laugh together,
easing the long day into the ginger night.

My grandma's there with us.

When the bonfire catches,
she tells us the sparks blink tiger-eyes
into the hanging dark.

And when a spray of flame traces a flare of burning logs
and embers flicker the marshmallow hour,
she starts singing,

> *Somewhere else a friend awaits,*
> *horses are riding wild across the ocean,*
> *stars are burning caves in a paper sky.*

My mum and dad go quiet then,
and everyone lingers in the silence.

Here on the beach,
we sit in a circle,
close,

already at the edge of far away.

FALL

Every October

　　my granddad used to say

　　　　On October mornings,
　　　　you can see figures in the fog—

　　　　giants, with no bones,
　　　　leaning sideways like old barn doors,
　　　　into patches of light—

　　　　or sometimes you can see black bears leaping,
　　　　playing black bear tag
　　　　where shadows twist in a cranberry bog—

　　　　by noon in the fall, they'll have cleared
　　　　　　away,
　　　　gone wherever holidays go,
　　　　after summer ends

Strata

I stopped one day
where a new road
sliced through a hillside,

and looked closely at the earth.
Layer by layer,
it told me its history:

white sediments of sea,
black rivers of leaf litter,
heat and decay:

I saw bright minerals—
red iron, yellow clay,
conglomerates of time,

and maybe a glacier's trail,
maybe a skeleton of shell—
slate, roots, or flint arrowheads.

Like cedar trees, ringing every year
their diaries of thirst and rain,
we belong to the earth, I realized.

Each day's a leaf,
each yesterday an oyster shell.
Every road we ride on lies on stone.

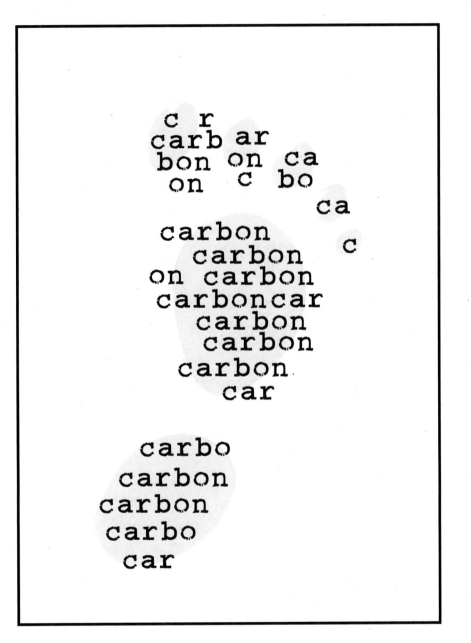

My Journal, November 1st

This week in school we had to write
something about Creatures from Outer Space
arriving on Earth, so I decided to write about
my brother. I called it Alien Visitors:

Every March from airless outer space
they drive
like maniacs: astro-mariners from the
planet Endive,

dissolved in green goddess dressing
or packed inside freeze-dried lettuce—

they're fluent in 73 languages, not
including Earth.
This year they came looking for olives.
"They're worth

a zillion krobneks on the planet
Radishwood,"
they said, in Radishwoodian, so nobody
except me understood.

"It's in the Celery Galaxy," they added,
which didn't help. My brother munched
his salad.

He didn't know someone was standing on
the edge of his plate,
watching him pick the tomatoes out.
He ate

everything else, crunching "bits that
tasted like clay,"
he said. I've wondered since if they
all got away—

the Olive-hunters, I mean—if so,
they left without saying *It's time to go*

in any one of the 73
languages they spoke to me—

I guess I'll have to stay perpetually
perplexed
till March, to find out what they'll be
looking for next—

I'm pretty sure it will be something
or other—
maybe my brother—

When I left a copy for him on his dinner plate, he told me that he'd had to write about outer space creatures, too, and that he wrote that I was actually covered in purple warts and was really a lizard that you could only see when I took off my Human Costume late at night. I told him Hallowe'en was over but if he wanted to see purple warts he could look in the mirror any time. My sister said "TCH" and tossed her head and tried to look bored. And then my mum and dad told us all to ACT OUR AGE! But we were only trying to have fun.

The carrots are almost all gone. I want to plant more next year.

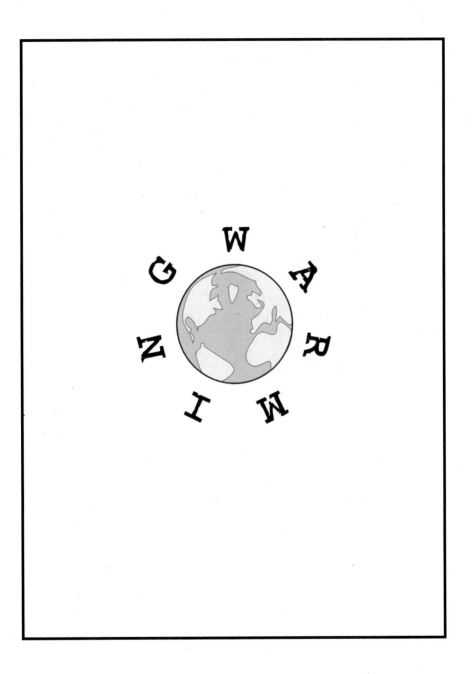

Particle Cycle

Fire Haiku

lightning bites: eats trees,
gnaws dry bark, flares into smoke,
chews needles, spits ash

*

Air Haiku

particles in air:
grit, smoke, car exhaust: even
fish hawks are coughing

Water Haiku

particles in rain:
dropping out of air onto
rivers, into earth

*

Earth Haiku

loam for blue roses:
sand for black castles: rock for
red opals, cold fire

A Handful of Earth

So take a scoop of earth in your hand.

Squeeze it. You're holding

one small corner of the world.

If you could take an acre, a city lot,

a hectare of rice, wheat, forest teak

or apple trees, would you toss it away?

The earth feeds you.

The forest gives you air to breathe.

Have they cut down all the trees?

THERAINFORESTTHERAINFOREST
THERAINFORESTTHERAINFOREST
THERAINFORESTTHERAINFOREST
THERAINFORESTTHERAINFOREST
THERAINFORESTTHERAINFOREST
THERAINFORESTTHERAINFOREST
THERAINFORESTTHERAINFOREST
THERAINFORESTTHERAINFOREST
THERAINFORESTTHERAINFOREST
THERAINFORESTTHERAINFOREST
THERAINFORESTTHERAINFOREST
THERAINFORESTTHERAINFOREST
THERAINFORESTTHERAINFOREST

THERAINFORESTTHERAINFOREST
THERAINFORESTTHERAINFOREST
THERAINFORESTTHERAINFOREST

c   g
h   n
o   i
p   p
p   p
i   o
n   h
g   c

STORES RAIN FOR FRESH AIR

SHARES STARS IN THE

NEAREST RAFTERS

STRIFE THREATEN S NESTS

STRESS STRAFE S STRAINS

ROTS ITS HEART

SHORT SHRIFT FOR SOFT FERNS

THIN RIFTS TEAR THERE

NOT FAIR TO FRITTER HERE,

RATS INFEST TREES

SHEAR FAST

THEN TOSS THE REST

FIRST HIT

STIRS A STA TE OF

FRO S T

AF

T

E

R

My Journal, December 1st

I don't tell everybody this, but I think I like thinking a whole lot, too. Last summer, kayaking on the lake, I spent a lot of time thinking about how things relate. How lines divide some things, for instance, but connect others. How numbers and words and musical notes all dance patterns. Why we understand words when we look at them or listen to them mumble and bellow and squawk and joke and sing.

I mean, I like thinking not just about the carrots I'm going to plant again next May but about how they grow as well—why they grow the way they do, and why they're good to eat. And about the ground they grow in, why it feeds us, and how we live. I want to know more about that.

My granddad liked to talk with me about
his garden.

This winter I'm learning to snowboard.

In Granddad's Garden

In granddad's garden,
carrots grow among the roses.

One tomato thrives beside the beans,
a second shoots up in the corn.

He reckoned people need fewer rows
to plant their dreams in,
and more supposing.

Maybe so.

I know I love the way that jungle beckoned
in granddad's garden.

Once a planting time ago,
I rambled footloose there—
no fungus-worry hurt, no fleck of fear.

When it's dark I trek there still,

but lightly now, dreaming slow
in granddad's garden.

Things I've Learned This Year

You can hold on to sunshine.

If you wear happiness around your shoulders
it will treat you like a parka,
and keep out the cold.

*

And you can hold on to clouds.

They'll carry you
past the skyline you think you see,
towards the one you dream.

Snow, too—you can hold on to snow.

It makes magic
out of maple trees
after the scarlet falls.

*

And if at night words threaten you
or separation chills, you can remember
you are stronger than the dark.

Hold on to the rain.

WINTER

I solved some puzzles, too.

Over the year I shared them all with my brother and sister. Some they figured out right away, and some they had to keep working at before they could decode them. But some of the others they said were JUST TOO HARD. When they said that, they were

```
        M          M          M          M
        A          A          A          A
M   D   M   D   M   D   M   D   M
A       A       A       A       A
D   ^   D   ^   D   ^   D   ^   D
```

But they got over it.